Acknowledgments

This book is dedicated to the men and women of fire departments everywhere who put themselves in harm's way to ensure the safety of their communities. Even though the firefighters of the Breezy Valley Fire Department may not look like those of your local fire department, great care has been taken to make certain that their methods and equipment reflect firefighting procedures in the human world.

Special thanks to Chief Gerald Bessette of the Barrington Fire Department for his insight and guidance. And to the Annapolis Fire Department for their kindness.
—RWA

Text and illustrations copyright © 2023 by R.W. Alley
All rights reserved. Copying or digitizing this book for storage, display,
or distribution in any other medium is strictly prohibited.

For information about permission to reproduce selections from this book, please contact
permissions@astrapublishinghouse.com.

Kane Press
An imprint of Astra Books for Young Readers, a division of Astra Publishing House
astrapublishinghouse.com
Printed in China

Library of Congress Cataloging-in-Publication Data
Names: Alley, R. W., 1955- author, illustrator.
Title: Firefighters to the rescue! / words and pictures by R. W. Alley.
Description: First edition. | New York : Kane Press, an imprint of Astra Books for Young Readers,
[2023] | A Breezy Valley at Work book– title page. | Audience: Ages 3-6 | Audience: Grades K-1 |
Summary: Firefighters to the rescue! The officers of Breezy Valley answer the call to protect
their beloved town. Ladders, axes, and water hoses take center stage as the firefighters rescue
the tabby cat twins, put out blazes, and save not only lives–but also the town ice cream parlor.
Lively action, equipment details, cross-section pictures and more will keep young firefighter
fans engaged throughout this delightful story.– Provided by publisher.
Identifiers: LCCN 2022061508 (print) | LCCN 2022061509 (ebook) | ISBN 9781662670275 (hc) |
ISBN 9781662670282 (eBook)
Subjects: LCSH: Fire extinction–Juvenile literature. | Fire fighters–Juvenile literature.
Classification: LCC TH9148.A35 2023 (print) | LCC TH9148 (ebook) | DDC 363.37–dc23/eng/20230320
LC record available at https://lccn.loc.gov/2022061508
LC ebook record available at https://lccn.loc.gov/2022061509
First edition

10 9 8 7 6 5 4 3 2 1

Design by Barbara Grzeslo
Logo design by Michelle Martinez
The text is set in Futura Std.
The speech bubble text is set in Kidprint bold.
The pictures, begun with pencils on a paper pad,
were finished up as pixels on an iPad.

BREEZY VALLEY

AT WORK

FIREFIGHTERS TO THE RESCUE!

Words and Pictures by

R.W. Alley

KANE PRESS

AN IMPRINT OF ASTRA BOOKS FOR YOUNG READERS

New York

It's a super breezy morning in Breezy Valley. A fresh crew of firefighters hurries to switch with yesterday's crew.

Each firefighter crew lives at the firehouse for a day and a night.

See you tomorrow morning!

BREEZY VALL
FIRE DEPART

BIG SCOOP
Home of the
Waffle Cone!

Stay safe!

The first thing the firefighters do is swap their street clothes for uniforms. Then they open their duty lockers where they keep their turnout gear. It super protects them in fires. They each have two sets.

They set up the gear in a special way. Boots tucked into pants. Suspenders ready for pulling on quick as a wink. Coat and helmet nearby.

Chief Piggie is in charge. When the crew's ready she reads out her checklist. Everyone has a job to do.

radio
antennas

satellite
dish →

BREEZY VALLEY
FIRE DEPARTMENT

Officer Puffin answers
9-1-1 calls and fire alarms
in the engine dispatch
center. Officer Gator
neatens the bunk room.

Big
Scoop

Down in the engine bays, Officer Fox polishes the
Pumper Engine and straightens the hoses. Officer Rabbit
greases the ladder slides on the Ladder Engine.

turnout gear

Suddenly,

Whoop! Whoop! Whoop!

There's trouble on Ripple Rock Ridge!

Officer Puffin grabs the headset and sounds the alarm.

BRAANNGG! BRAANNGG! BRAANNGG!

The officers scramble into their turnout gear. It weighs forty-five pounds!

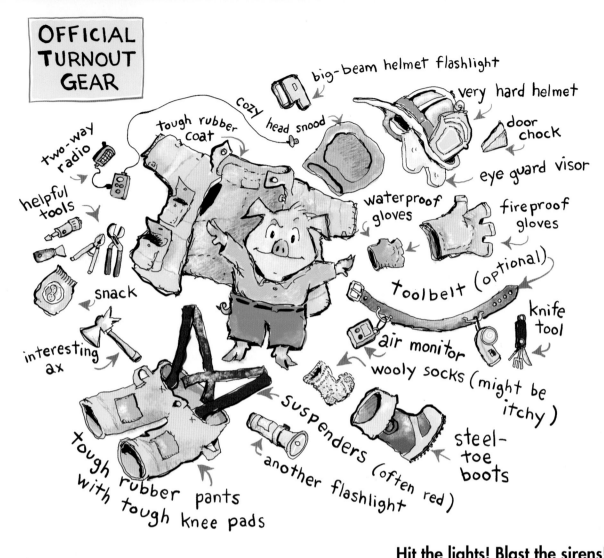

OFFICIAL TURNOUT GEAR

big-beam helmet flashlight

very hard helmet

cozy head snood

door chock

tough rubber coat

two-way radio

eye guard visor

helpful tools

waterproof gloves

fireproof gloves

snack

toolbelt (optional)

knife tool

interesting ax

air monitor

wooly socks (might be itchy)

suspenders (often red)

steel-toe boots

another flashlight

tough rubber pants with tough knee pads

Hit the lights! Blast the sirens!
Firefighters to the rescue!

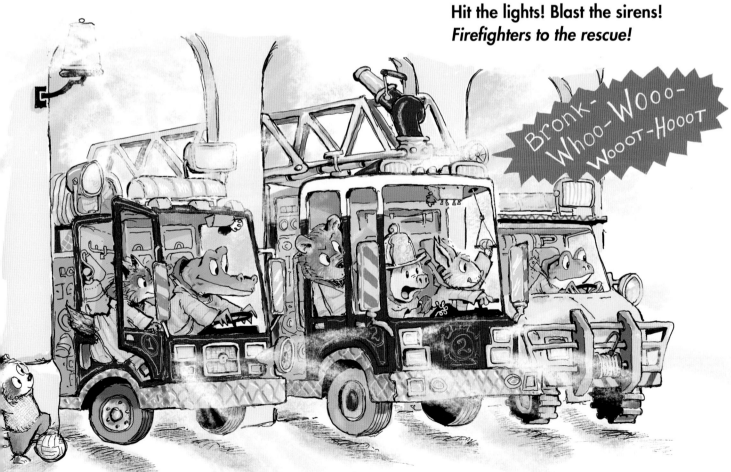

Bronk-Whoo-Wooo-Wooot-Hooot

The Pumper Engine leads the way!

PUMPER ENGINE – *outside and inside*

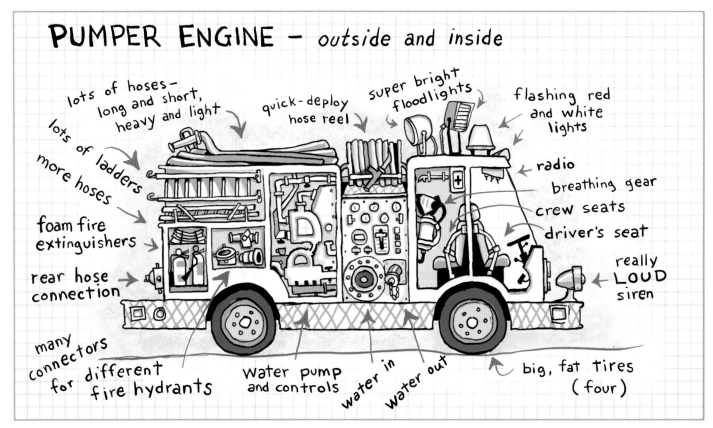

lots of hoses—
long and short,
heavy and light

quick-deploy
hose reel

super bright
floodlights

flashing red
and white
lights

lots of ladders

more hoses

foam fire
extinguishers

rear hose
connection

radio

breathing gear

crew seats

driver's seat

really
LOUD
siren

many
connectors
for different
fire hydrants

water pump
and controls

water in

water out

big, fat tires
(four)

MAIN St

whee-wooo-whee-wooo-whee-woooo

Then comes the Ladder Engine.

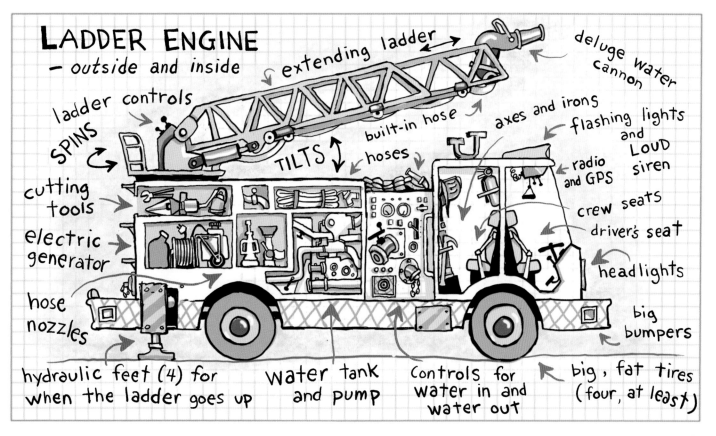

LADDER ENGINE
— outside and inside

extending ladder →

deluge water cannon

ladder controls

built-in hose

axes and irons

flashing lights and LOUD siren

SPINS

TILTS ↕

hoses

radio and GPS

crew seats

cutting tools

driver's seat

electric generator

headlights

hose nozzles

big bumpers

hydraulic feet (4) for when the ladder goes up

water tank and pump

Controls for water in and water out

big, fat tires (four, at least)

WOOOT-HOOOT
WOOOT-HOOOT
WOOOT-HOOOT

Then comes the Brush-Breaker Truck.
Everyone gets out of the way. The firefighters zip and zoom,
twisting and turning through Breezy Valley.

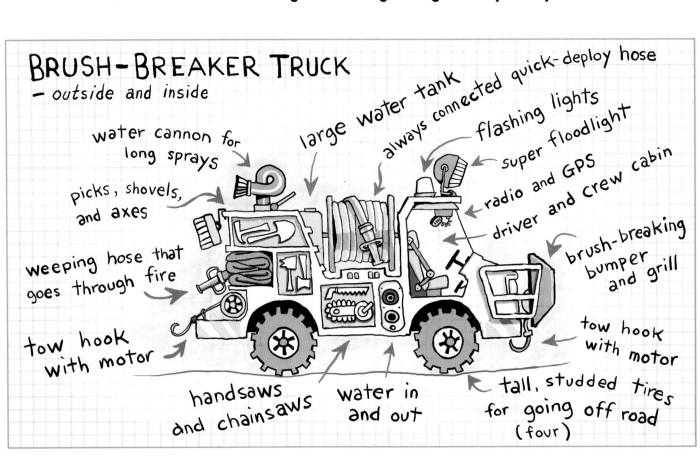

BRUSH-BREAKER TRUCK
— outside and inside

large water tank

always connected quick-deploy hose

flashing lights

super floodlight

radio and GPS

driver and crew cabin

water cannon for
long sprays

picks, shovels,
and axes

brush-breaking
bumper
and grill

weeping hose that
goes through fire

tow hook
with motor

tow hook
with motor

handsaws
and chainsaws

water in
and out

tall, studded tires
for going off road
(four)

The Tabby Twins are perilously perched. The firefighters know what to do!

Up slides the Ladder Engine ladder. Up scamper officers Toad, Rabbit, and Fox. Officer Gator works the controls. Down come the Tabby Twins, safe and sound.

Officers Rabbit, Bear, and Gator strap into their breathing gear. It weighs thirty pounds!

OFFICIAL SELF-CONTAINED BREATHING APPARATUS or SCBA for short

air cylinder or tank

trusty helmet

whole-face breathing mask goes under trusty helmet

thick, clear-plastic face guard

back-pack with lots of buckles and belts

regulator controls air flow

air hose

super strong light to cut through smoke

ax and halligan for smashing through doors and walls

air pressure gauge

Same turnout gear and boots

Chief Piggie and Officers Fox and Toad hook up the hoses between the fire hydrant and the Pumper Engine.

water pumped OUT super fast by pump inside engine

snazzy spray nozzle — pull back handle to work

fire hydrant

twist nut left to open

water into engine

check valve

always full, underground pipes connect all the hydrants

First, from up high, Chief Piggie soaks Big Scoop with the deluge cannon.

Then Officer Gator chops a hole in the roof above the hottest spot of the fire. The smoke blows up and out.

Officers Bear and Rabbit run hose lines from below and blast the flames with a combo mix of water and foam. Officer Fox watches for flying sparks.

The firefighters crawl and poke with their irons. They douse every pocket of smoke. Big Scoop is sopping wet, but the firefighters stay dry in their turnout gear.

At last, the kitchen fire puffs out.

But . . .

Oh, no! Blown by the breeze, a red-hot
ember sparks the tall grass in the
meadow next door!

Chief Piggie drives the Brush-Breaker
Truck deep into the meadow.
It has its own water tank.
The firefighters surround the fire.

Officer Toad uses a special weeping hose that
goes through fire without burning up.

Officers Fox and Rabbit scrape away the dry meadow grass so the flames can't jump and spread. They smother stray embers with dirt.

We've got it surrounded!

After the fires have fizz-fizzled out, the firefighters overhaul the scene for hot spots. Then they roll up the hoses and twist shut the fire hydrant.

Lion wants to thank them with cold, cool Coconut Surprise.
But it's all melted.

Then Penguin has a wonderful good idea.

Back at the Breezy Valley Firehouse, there's more to do.

The firefighters put their smokey turnout gear in the wash. They scrub the soot and muck off the engines and truck. Exhaust removal hoses go on the tailpipes for when the motors run inside the building. They roll out the fire hoses to drain and dry.

Finally and most importantly, the firefighters set up their second set of turnout gear. Everything must be ready for the next alarm.

exhaust removal hoses

switching out empty air tanks

fresh hoses

to the laundry

Now the firefighters can
scrub themselves.

The officers put on fresh uniforms.
Officer Rabbit challenges
Office Puffin to checkers.

Officer Bear needs some quiet book
time in the bunk room.

Officer Toad whips up some more
snacks, even though they're all pretty
full from Coconut Surprise soup.

But . . .

before anyone can take a bite,

Whoop! Whoop! Whoop!

Officer Puffin grabs the microphone and sounds the alarm.

Car crash on Fairgrounds Road!

BRAANNGG! BRAANNGG! BRAANNGG!

The officers scramble into their fresh turnout gear and onto their clean engines and trucks.

Hit the lights! Blast the sirens!
Firefighters to the rescue!

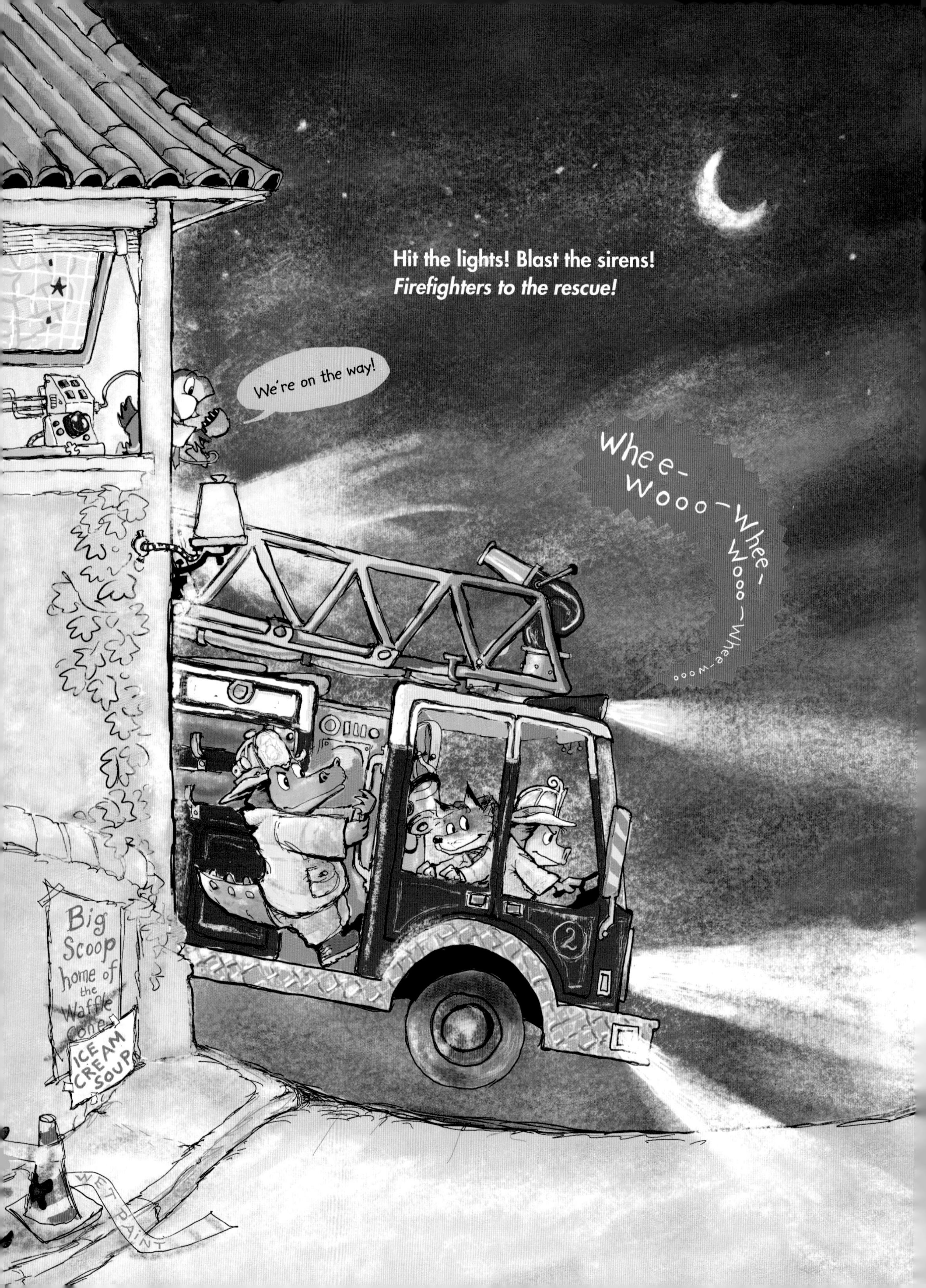

Join the crew!

Have you noticed Dog following the firefighters?
Dog is a reporter with a nose for news and a camera to snap it.
Can you find the pages where Dog snapped these pictures?

Between alarms, what's on Chief Piggie's to-do list?

☐ **Check the smoke alarms at Breezy Valley School.**

☐ **Flush the fire hydrants.**

☐ **Take newly charged fire extinguisher to Betty's Buttery Bakery.**

Can you find Big Scoop, Breezy Valley School, six fire hydrants, and Betty's Buttery Bakery on the Breezy Valley map?

Some fire emergencies are hard to reach with engines and trucks.

In Breezy Valley, a Fire Boat responds to trouble near or on the water.

A Fire Copter can dump chemicals or water on blazes up in the hills and forests where there aren't roads. Can you spy the special firehouses for the Fire Boat and the Fire Copter on the Breezy Valley map?